T0165156

WADE
JACKSON

Christopher Veasley

Order this book online at www.trafford.com
or email orders@trafford.com

Most Trafford titles are also available at major online book retailers.

Printed in the United States of America.

ISBN: 978-1-4269-9544-6 (sc)
ISBN: 978-1-4269-9545-3 (e)

Trafford rev. 09/16/2011

 www.trafford.com

North America & international
toll-free: 1 888 232 4444 (USA & Canada)
phone: 250 383 6864 ♦ fax: 812 355 4082

Wade's first Job

(Introduction)

"Hi, my name is Wade Jackson and this is my story."
"I was born and raised in Arkansas on November 12, 1993 by my mother Lisa McCool. She's a nurse, she works at the children's hospital. My father, Benny Jackson works as a sales manager at a car dealership. My father and mother got into a disagreement on wheather or not I'm his son. Well, my mother and father did sleep together a couple of months later after they've met. We all know what happens when a man and a woman share the same bed, let's say magic was in the air that night. When my mother told dad that she was pregnant, he started to flip out, he was angry. He said to her "that child is not mine" and she said "you were the only man I was with that night when we made love, so how can you deny that this child isn't yours?"

"It's not my kid, the plan was to get some that night, not make a baby" , Benny said.

"It took a few minutes for my mother to figure out my father and why he did what he did."

"So you slept with me to feel happy about yourself and brag about it with your friends?"

"Yeah, I'ma player and players don't just sleep with one only woman and they damn sure don't make babies" , Benny said with anger in his voice. "My mother was in disbelief that day, she was shocked. She couldn't believe what my father was saying to her."

"The whole time when my mother and father was together as a couple, dad been lying to her about loving her, taking good care of her and always being there by her side. "Dad said all that just to have sex with her, and now that she was pregnant with me, he didn't want anything to do with her and me."

"You get the HELL out of my house and my life benny, I don't ever want to see you again," Lisa shouted.

"Dad left her house and drove off. Mother was still in disbelief, she broke down in tears."

"My mother told me that story when I was fourteen years old, but I still haven't seen my dad."

"Three years later, I was forgetting about my dad and stayed focus on my school work."

"Now that I'm done with my final exams for my junior in Emerson high school, I can now focus on my job and Its my first one," Wade said.

"I started this job the same week as my exams. I work part time, from five o' clock to nine o' clock. I walk to work, I don't live far from it.

"One of the supervisors helped me get started, his name is Mike Hitmen. He's tall, he looks like he's in his thirties and he seem pretty cool, but he's not my supervisor. I asked him "who is my supervisor?"

Mrs. Loretta styles is. She's not here today, but I'll tell her about you when I see her," he said.

"I started work on a Friday, so I'll meet Mrs. styles on Monday. So, Mr. Hitmen showed me everything I needed to do."

"He showed me the restrooms, the windows that needed to be cleaned, the carpets that needed to be vacuumed and where to take out the trash."

"After work, I went home and mom asked "how was day at work?"

"Cleaning, and a whole lot of it. Its easy though, its not hard. I clean all the restrooms on all five floors, the windows on the first and second floor and vacuum the carpets."

"How many restrooms did you clean on all five floors?" Lisa asked.

"There's three on each floor, so its fifteen in all. I clean the men's, women's and handicap's," wade said.

I took out all the trash after everthing else was finished on all floors."

"You think you can handle the responsibilties of that job all summer long?" Lisa asked.

"Yeah, It's not that bad."

"Who's your supervisor?" Lisa asked.

"Mrs. Loretta styles, she wasn't there today, I'll meet her Monday. Mr. Hitmen showed me everything, he's a another supervisor who works there." Wade explained.

"Well, at least your working somewhere, congratulations, I'm proud of you baby," Lisa said with a smile.

"Thank you, now, I'm about to go relax and watch WWE Friday Night Smackdown!

A New Look

" During the summer, I did my best to lose weight. Ever since I started school, I had people pick on me about my weight. Some of them tell jokes like, "wade so fat, he got more meat on him than any supermarket combined" or wade's body so big, it looks like he'e going to rip out of his clothes like the Incredible Hulk."

" The more I think about those jokes, the angrier I get.

The person I really hate is this guy name Jimmy Sailor, his friends calls him Mack. He's been bothering me since we met and he's also the quarterback on the football team. He has a girlfriend whose on the cheerleading squad, drill team actually, her name is Angel Brown. Now, I got to focus on the future and how to lose weight."

"I started to think long and hard, I was determined to do whatever it took to lose a couple of pounds, I wanted to look different before my senior year came back. I started to think about buying workout equipments and food that'll help shred some body fat. I made a list of everything I needed so I won't forget. That same day, I saw a commercial about a Bowflex home gym and I thought about ordering one by using my mother's credit card, I had to ask first."

"After I came home from work, mother and I went to the grocery store. She said "grab anything you like to eat."

"So I grab anything that would help me lose weight, diet sodas to slim fast to salads and even yogurts. My mother notice that this isn't the food I usually eat. She said "These are all weight lost food, are you sure you want me to purchase it?"

"I told her yes and I told her I'm trying to lose weight this summer. I told her that I'm sticking with this plan everyday, and I meant it."

"Let's get the rest of the food and check out," Lisa said. Afterwards, Wade and Lisa sat down and had an discussion after coming home from the grocery store. "How was your day?" Lisa asked.

"I just went to work to see if we work on weekends, I forgot to ask them that and I guess he forgot to tell me."

"What did he say?" Lisa asked.

"No, we don't work weekends. Can I ask a favor of you?"

"Yeah, what?" Lisa said.

"Can I use your credit card to order a Bowflex machine?"

"Why do you need that?" she asked.

"I think it helps burn fat a lot faster if I just keep at it, everbody said so."

"How much is it gonna cost?" Lisa asked.

"Not much, just thirty nine dollars a month."

"Sure, why not. When you gonna call them?" Lisa asked.

"Well, actually I was hoping on that you would call them because you have to be eighteen or older."

"Really? I'll call them tomorrow," Lisa said.

"I really appreciate my mother that day when she agreed to order me a bowflex. The next day she called and ordered it, it was going to take time for it to arrive here, so I started doing other exercises. I did push ups, but not that many because I was heavy, but I kept at it. I started to walk around the neighborhood a couple of times, I'd walk for thirty minutes. Afterwards, mother asked me "why do you want to lose weight all of a sudden?"

I thought to myself, I wanted to show off my abs and muscles to the ladies and make everybody else feel like punks and pathectic."

"Wade? do you hear me? are you daydreaming again?" Lisa asked.

"I just told her that I'm trying to be healthy and eat healthy."

Chapter 3

Stick to your goals

"Remember to lock the door before leaving for work," Lisa said.

"Alright, I will," wade said.

Lisa got in her car and drove off to work.

"I had all morning to myself, so I continued to stick to my goal. I started my day off by doing push ups and jumping jacks. Then, I went for another walk. Later on that day, I met my supervisor at work, she's pretty nice. She asked me "Did Mr. Hitmen show you everything?" I told her yes. So, I got started with my work. I swept, mopped, vaccumed, clean the windows and took out the trash on all five floors. Everyday I start on the fourth floor because that's where my cart is to roll around to clean everything. Then, I go up to the fifth floor and work my way back down."

"The job isn't hard, all we do is clean up the place. Mrs. styles told me to mop the lobby two days per week instead of doing it everyday, I was relieved when she told me that."

"I finished pretty early." After cleaning everything, Wade decided to take a break. "I still got five minutes to spare, I got done with my work early" , wade said. Five minutes pass and wade went to lock the storage room and unlock the elevator. Then, he went to go clock out and sign out and walked home.

Notice a change

The next morning, Wade woked up and then freshen up before his daily routine. Lisa had already left for work and wade started to notice he had hair growing under his chin. He took a closer look and he also notice that a mustage is growing. "Mom is not going to believe this once I tell her" , wade said. Later on that day, a delivery package came for Lisa. Since Lisa was at work, wade signed for her. "I need you to sign here please," the man said. "Thank you, he said, now, where do you want it?"

"What is it?" Wade asked. "A bowflex workout machine," he said. "Set it in this room," wade said. The delivery man brung the machine in the same room wade is using for a home gym. After the man left, wade was excited. The bowflex finally came and he started to read the instructions first, before he tried it out. "I'll tell momma about it if she doesn't know it's here," wade said. For the next twenty minutes, wade started to workout on the bowflex. Afterwards, he took a break and then later on that day, he went to work.

"Hey," the security guard said when wade walk up to the counter to sign in. "Hi," wade responded back to her. Wade walked down the hallway to the janitorial room to pick up his keys and clocked in. "What's going on Mr. Jackson?" Mr. Hitmen said with excitement. "Nothing much, Wade said. Same thing everyday."

"And what's that?" Mr. Hitmen asked. "Working out to lose weight and eating healthy."

"I hear ya, Mr. Hitmen said. It's important to stay healthy as long as you can and working out can help you lose weight also."

"Yeah, Wade agreed. I got that new bowflex machine today and I'ma buy some more workout equipments on Saturday."

"How it worked out for you?" Mr. Hitmen asked. "I was feeling some pain in both my arms, so I guess it was working, I stayed on it for twenty minutes."

"O.k." Mr. Hitmen said, but you have to use that machine three times a day don't ya?"

"Yeah, I only used it once today because I had to get ready to come to work. I'ma get back on it once I go home for another twenty minutes."

"Alright, Mr. Hitmen said, keep doing what your doing, you'll lose the weight that you want to lose." After the conversation, wade went to work. After finishing the job for today, Wade went home and told his mother about the bowflex. "The bowflex came today," wade said.

"Where is it?" Lisa asked. Wade opened the door. "Right here" , wade said. Lisa, with a smile on her face said "Wow, look how good it looks. Have you tried it out yet?"

"Yeah, Wade responded. It works pretty good."

"Alright, Lisa said. Take it easy on it, we don't want you pullin' a muscle!"

Wade started to workout again for another twenty minutes. Day by day, wade stayed focus on loosing weight and focusing on his job everyday.

Chapter 5

Goal Achieved

"I lost a total of twenty four pounds, wade said. I used to weigh two hundred eight, now, I weigh one eighty four. I have achieved my goal for this summer, but I'm goin' to continue to eat healthy and stick to my workout plans."

Wade was happy that he lost that weight and gained twenty nine pounds of muscles. He can now do more sit ups and push ups than he did in the beginning. "There's only one month before school, I guess I'm going to continue what I'm doin' now. I need to ask momma to take me shopping for some clothes and shoes." After work that day, wade went home and asked his mother, Lisa to take him shopping. She said yes, she'll take him on Saturday. "School is coming back so soon?" Lisa asked. "Yeah, Wade responded. I'm just glad that this is my last year."

"This is my last time getting registared in school, walking back and forth to school, taking quizes, tests, and exams."

"Have you ever thought about what your going to do after high school?" Lisa asked.

"No, I haven't thought that far ahead, I was going to think about that later on."

"What you do if you had to pick right now?" Lisa asked. Wade started to think. "I want to go to the NAVY, they help you out with anything and they help pay for college. Right now, I don't think we can afford college on our own," Wade said.

"What would you do in the NAVY if you got in?" Lisa asked. "I thought about doing auto technology, where you learn how to fix cars. There's other opportunities you can do in the NAVY, but auto technology is all I have on my mind right now when I think about joining the NAVY. I got plenty of time to think about all that, right now, I'm focus on finishing high school."

A few weeks later, Lisa took wade to go get registared for the last time. A few days later, wade continued to workout everyday and go to work everyday. On saturday he went to the barbershop called "Razor Edge" where he can get a haircut for up to fifteen dollars. "How much for an all even razor cut?" Wade asked.

"Fifteen dollars," the barber said.

"O.k. can you give me that haircut?" Wade asked.

"Yeah, no problem. Is this your first time here?" the barber asked.

"Yeah," Wade responded.

"What's your name little man?"

"Wade"

"My name's Kyle. You in school?"

"Yeah, I go to Emerson high school and this is my last year there."

"Alright that's good, Kyle said. What you plan on doing after graduation?"

"I want to go to the NAVY so I can study auto technology."

"Like, working on cars?" Kyle asked.

"Yeah."

"O.k. what you been doing for the summer?" Kyle asked.

"Working as a janitor and working out." Wade responded.

"Was there a reason for you to be working out? or you just love to do it?" Kyle asked.

"There's a reason. I'm trying to lose as much weight as I can before school came back and it looks like I did just that."

"Congratulations young man on accomplishing your goal," kyle said.

"Thank you. The next thing I want to do is working on getting my permit so I can start driving."

"How old are you?" Kyle asked.

"Seventeen."

"Yeah, your old enough to start learning. All you need to do is study the Arkansas Driver License study guide booklet and take a test on it, once you've pass, you'll get your permit."

"Yeah, I'm goin' to ask my momma can she teach me how to drive after I go get a study guide on driving. And studying it so I can pass the knowledge test. If I do get my driver's license, I need my own car. I'm thinkin' bout askin' my uncle can I borrow his car to drive in until I have enough money to buy my own.

"How many vehicles does your uncle have?" Kyle asked.

"Two, he has one car and one truck. I'm thinking about asking him for the car because he loves to drive his truck more than he drives his car."

"So, he's more of a trucker?" Kyle asked.

"Yeah, he's a mechanic too, so whenever his truck or car isn't working properly, he'll get right on it to make it work properly again. How much for the haircut again?" Wade asked.

"Fifteen dollars," kyle said.

"Alright Kyle, I appreciate the cut, I'll come back again next time," wade said after shaking hands with Kyle.

"I appreciate you for stopping by, yeah, come back again and let me know how things are going," Kyle said.

"I'll do that," Wade said.

Wade went home and started to wash his head to get out all the extra hair that was left in his head. Afterwards, he decided to play some video games.

Chapter 6

First day of school

"Today's the first day, I wonder how this will turn out," wade said after waking up from bed.

"Wade? Lisa hollered. Breakfast is on the table and don't be late for school. I'm on my way to work."

After Lisa left, Wade was getting ready for the first day of school. After breakfast, he locked up the door after he went out and headed to school. "I wonder whats on my schedule this year. I hope I got some classes that I can pass because I'm tryin' to graduate and be done with high school."

Wade arrived at Emerson high school and got in line to get his schedule. Once wade received his schedule, he read it. "First block is, Mr. Webster for English, second block is African American History with Mr. Jones and Third block is geometry with Miss. Berrie. All those classes is for "A" days which is today and for "B" days I have P.E. for first block with coach Phillip, second block is Art with Ms. Dixon, and third block is Nutrition and Wellness class with Mrs. Young."

"What's up wade?" Wade turned around.

"Hey, what's up Lamman? what's goin' on?"

They both shooked hands and smiled. "Nothin' much, Lamman said. I just been workin' all summer mostly. My parents and I came back in town Friday, we went to Hot Springs for my little cousin birthday party and we stayed there for a few days just to be around family before I had to come back to school. What have you been up to during the summer vacation?" Lamman asked.

"Workin' at this new job I got and losing weight," Wade said.

"You do look like you've lost a lot of weight, Lamman said. How much you lost?"

"Twenty four pounds," Wade answered.

"What did you do to lose weight?" Lamman asked.

"I ate healthy food that'll help a person lose weight and I worked out on the bowflex machine that my momma bought me." Lamman nodded his head. "Hold on, let me change the subject for a minute," he said.

"What new job are you workin' at?"

"It's a janitorial job, Wade said. I started in the summer and I still work there."

"That's cool, Lamman said. I mean, it's better than having no job at all."

"I heard that, Wade said. Who do you have for today and tomorrow?"

"I have Mr. Webster for English, Mr. Jones for African American History and Miss Berrie for Geometry for "A" days. For "B" days, I have P.E. with coach phillip, Art with Ms. Dixon and Nutrition wellness with Mrs. Young."

"It looks like we have the same classes everyday, you have all the classes I have on my schedule," Wade said.

"Finally, Lamman said. All the years we known each other, we never had the same classes everyday. Know what? this is are last time lookin' out for each other, for school that is, this is the last time for us to have each other's backs while in school."

"Yeah, wade said. You're right, and since this is our last year, we need to make the most out of it."

Lamman nodded his head. "When you say make the most out of it, do you mean we go to school dances, prom or I don't know, make perfect attendance?" Lamman asked.

"Yeah, something like that, I just want something to look back on in the next few years," Wade said.

"I hear ya," Lamman said.

"One more thing too, wade said. I never got the chance to say that I appreciate you taking up for me for the last three years from all those kids that's been picking on me, especially Mack. Mack's been firing me up ever since the ninth grade."

"His real name is Jimmy sailor, Lamman said. His friends calls him Mack because of his way with the ladies and since we're not his friends, we call him Jimmy."

Chapter 7

Maxine and Sonya

The bell ranged and Wade and Lamman went to their first class. They met their teacher, Mr.Webster and were assigned at the table at the back of the classroom on the left side. "I'm glad we're at the back of the classroom 'cause I don't like sittin' in the front or middle in any classroom," wade said.

"I'm with you on that," Lamman said. "To me, it's uncomfortable 'cause most kids play too much. They throw paper balls, paper clips or eraser's from a pencilat you when your not looking. It just makes you mad 'cause it's hard to concentrate on the assignment when you got high school kids being like elementary kids throwing things at you."

"Yeah, that's true," wade said. Let's hope that Mr. Webster doesn't give us new seats this entire year."

"Look who we have here," Lamman said. It's Angel brown and her best friend Aja chambers."

"I didn't know they had this class," wade said.

"I don't like neither of them," Lamman said.

"Yeah, me too, wade said. They hang out with Jimmy and you know I don't like him."

"Jimmy and Angel are dating," Lamman said. They got together close to the end of the last few weeks of last year, our junior year."

"I haven't notice," Wade said. I don't pay attention to what jimmy is doin'. Then entered two more people that wade and Lamman is familiar with. "Maxine Rogers and Sonya Tower have this class too?" Wade asked.

"Yeah, it looks like it, Lamman said. I'm gonna ask Mr. Webster can they sit at the in front of us or next to us."

Lamman did so and Mr.Webster asked why. "Is there a reason of why you want Miss Rogers and Miss Tower to sit next to you?"

"I know them," Lamman said. I'm not going to cause any distractions."

"If I see you talking while I'm talking, I will assign you to another table up front," Mr. Webster told Lamman.

"Yeah, alright I hear what ya saying," Lamman said.

Mr. Webster assigned Maxine and Sonya to the table next to wade's and Lamman's. Once the bell ranged, Mr. Webster introduced himself to the class and started to call rows. Afterwards, he gave everyone their assignments on writing skills in an handbooklet. Sonya looked over to Wade's and Lamman's table. "Hi, Lamman, she said. Wade? is that you?"

"Yeah, it's me, wade responded."

Maxine looked over and joined the conversation. "Hey Lamman, she said. Is that wade over there too?"

"Yeah, this is him. So, what you two been up to?" Lamman asked.

"Summer was the best this year, Sonya said. I got my driver's license finally and now I can work full time at my job."

"You still work at K-Mart?" Lamman asked.

"Yep, I'm also looking for a second job."

"That's what's up. Maxine? what you been up to?"

"My summer vacation is or should I say was similar to Sonya's. I got my driver's license as well and I already got two jobs."

"What two jobs you got?" Lamman asked.

"My first job is at Red Lobster and my second is at Kroger."

"That's what's up," Lamman said.

"What about you? Sonya asked. What you been up to?"

"Workin' mostly, I got a job too," Lamman said.

"Where?" Maxine asked.

"At subway, Lamman responded. I'm lookin' for a second job too. I already filled out a couple of applications, I'm just waitin' on a phone call from one of those companies."

"That's good that ya'll got your license, but do ya'll have a car?" Lamman asked.

"Yeah, I do, Sonya said. It's a two thousand Chevy Malibu. My dad helped me buy it from one of his friends who was selling it for three thousand and one hundred eighty five dollars. I put five hundred on it to help purchase it," said sonya.

"My mom and dad said they were going to buy me a car either for my birthday or christmas, Maxine said. That's good, but I don't know what kind of car they plan to buy me."

"Until then, you can ride with me. You know I got your back, you know we're like sisters."

Maxine smiled. "Thank you, give me a hug."

"That's very thoughtful of you Sonya, said Wade. Not a lot of people will say that to a friend to help them out whenever they need help. Keep your friendship strong, don't let some bull crap come between your friendship. Bull crap like some "he say, she say" stuff that may not be true. What I'm sayin' is, don't believe some things that other people might tell you. For example, if Sonya says something negative about Maxine if someone told Maxine what Sonya said. Don't belive that person until you two talk to each other about it to find out if its true or not.

"I know what your sayin' Lamman said. My man Wade speaks the truth, the whole truth and nothin' but the truth."

It's been a lot of bull crap spreading around this school like a virus, somebody lying on another just to get entertained," Maxine said.

"That's true," Sonya said.

The bell ranged for everyone to go to their next classroom. "Let's talk some more outside," Maxine said.

"O.k," Wade responded.

The Confrontation

Wade and Lamman both went to Mr. Jones room for African American History class. After meeting Mr. Jones and their classmates and working on their assignments, the bell ranged for lunch. Then, wade mt up with Maxine outside at the table. "Hey wade," Maxine said with a smile.

"Hey, Wade responded. Where's Sonya?"

"She's with Lamman over at the other table having a private conversation."

"You know Lamman likes Sonya," wade said.

"And Sonya likes Lamman. I wonder when one of them is going to ask the other one out," Maxine said.

"Why don't you have a boyfriend?" Wade asked.

"Some of the guys I meet is not my type, some of them are mean, nasty and disrespectful. I can't be around those kind of boys. I want someone that could treat her right, protect me, like me, love me, hold me, accept me for who I am, support me and always be there for me and never leave me alone by myself. Is that too much to ask for?" Maxine asked.

"It is when you think about it, heh, heh, heh, heh, heh," Wade said with a smile making jokes.

"Shut up," Maxine said while giggling.

"Seriously though, I hear what your saying, a good man is hard to find," Wade said.

"Yeah, and why don't you have a girlfriend?" Maxine asked.

"I don't know, I guess I haven't found the right one yet," wade responded.

"Really?" Maxine asked.

"Yeah, I wouldn't know miss right if I'm lookin' right at her," Wade said.

"No kidding," Maxine said with a smile.

"What's that suppose to mean?" Wade asked with a smile.

"I know what your saying?"

"Oh yeah, Maxine said. What?"

"Your sayin' your Miss right," Wade said.

"Even if I am saying that, would you go out with me?" Maxine asked with a smile.

"Well, hypothetically speaking, what would happen if I said yes?" Wade asked.

"Well, I would be happy, we would go out to dinner or a movie, we would call each other, we would celebrate birthdays and holidays together and I would lean over this table and kiss you," Maxine said.

"What if I said no?" Wade asked.

"You would break my heart," Maxine said.

"We can't have that, wade said with a smile. And yes, I would be happy to go out with you."

Maxine smiled with joy. They both leaned over the table and kissed.

"Your a good kisser," Maxine said.

"Really? it wasn't bad, sloppy, too much lip?" Wade asked.

"No silly," Maxine said while smiling.

"I'll be back with a contract tomorrow to make this relationship official alright?" Wade said while smiling.

Maxine laughs at Wade's jokes.

"What are your plans after high school?" Maxine asked.

"Long term, I want to go to the NAVY and do auto technology so I can work on auto mobile, you know, how to fix on them when something goes wrong. Short term, I want to be a writer. I'm pretty good at writing stories and writing poetry."

"Oooh, I love poetry, I've read a few books on poetry before," Maxine said.

"I got a few papers on poetry that I've written back in seventh and eighth grade that I've kept and I got some that I've written recently," Wade said.

"I haven't written any stories yet, I still got the ones I written back in seventh, eighth and tenth grade. It turns out that I'm pretty good at writing, I figure if my teachers and classmates likes them, then why not write a few stories and poetry for the whole world to read," Wade said.

"Can I read a few of your poetry papers?" Maxine asked.

"Yeah, why not? I'll bring them tomorrow, I think you'll like them once you read 'em. What's your plans after high school Maxine?" Wade asked.

"I want to be an actress, Maxine responded. I didn't think I could act until I performed on stage in drama class with my group and my teacher said I did a good job acting out my part. Since then, I did well in all my other performances and I soon realize that acting can become a career of mine one day. My back up plan is becoming a nurse if acting doesn't work out. I want to help save lives from danger like HIV, viruses, disease, stuff like that, cancer also."

"Cool," Wade said. "I'll stand behind you and show support in your journey to become an actress or nurse?"

"Thank you Wade," Maxine said.

"Wade? Maxine called him. Give me a hug, that is so nice on what you said. They both hugged. Wade turned his head and here comes Mack sailor.

"Oh hell no," Wade said with anger.

"Whats wrong?" Maxine asked.

"Mack's coming over here."

"Maybe he won't notice us," Maxine said.

"Hey guy," Mack said. Have I seen you before?"

"I don't think so," Wade responded.

"It feels like I know you . . . Wade Jackson! right?"

"So it is you, you lost weight, how much? fifty tons?"

Mack and his crew started to laugh. Wade feels embarrassed and humiliated. Then, Wade stood up and responded.

"Why don't you leave me alone and go on about your business?"

"What's gonna happen if I don't?" Mack asked.

"You'll find out sooner than you think punk," Wade said.

"Hey, hey, hey that's enough, let's go Wade," Maxine said.

"No, I'm not going anywhere, we was here first, I'm not about to move somewhere else just because his punk ass came over here, he needs to leave," Wade said.

"You better watch your mouth fool," Mack said angrily.

Lamman saw what was happening and got between Mack and wade to settle things down.

"Come on Wade, don't fight him, it's the first day of school, it's too early for all this drama," Lamman said.

"Come on baby, don't waste your time on him," Angel said.

Mack and his crew left. Wade was still angry.

"That dude is wack, Lamman said. First day of school and he's already picking on people."

"You o.k Wade?" Sonya asked.

"Yeah, I'll be fine, thanks."

Meanwhile, Mack and his crew are having an discussion.

"Usually he don't say anything when someone talks bad about him, Sean said. I guess that he lost weight, he feels high and mighty, you know, he's the man."

"I'll find out how good he really is later on this year, now is too early," Mack said.

"What do you think their talking about?" Maxine said.

"Probably about me as always, Wade said. I really don't give a damn, as long as neither one of them puts their hands on me, they can talk as much as they want."

The bell ranged and it was time for third block.

"Who do you got next Maxine?" Wade asked.

"Mr. Jones for African American History."

"Lamman and I had that class before lunch today," wade said.

"How was it?" Maxine asked.

"Fine, Mr. Jones seems pretty cool," Wade said.

"Who do you have next?" Maxine asked.

"Miss Berrie for geometry. Lamman's in there too," wade said.

"I have to go, I'll see you later right?" Maxine asked.

"Yeah, I'll catch up with you later," wade said.

"Alright, bye," Maxine said.

"Bye," Wade responded.

"Where you going to next?" Sonya asked Lamman.

"I got geometry with Wade in Miss. Berrie's class.

"Who you got next?" Lamman asked.

"African American History with Maxine in Mr. Jones class," Sonya said.

"Alright then, I'll talk to you later," Lamman said.

"Give me a hug before you go," Sonya said.

They both hugged and then went to class. Lamman met up with Wade at class.

"What's up Wade, it's a good thing I made it here on time," Lamman said.

"Where were you?" Wade asked.

"With Sonya."

The bell ranged and Miss. Berrie introduced herself to the class and called row. Then, she gaved everyone their assignment.

"If you don't know a problem or two, don't hesitate to come up and ask me," she said.

"There are only ten problems on this sheet that I want all of you to solve," Miss. Berrie said.

Wade raised his hand for a question. "Yes, do you have a question?"

"Do we take this home for homework if we don't finished or turn in what we've done so far?"

"Take it with you for homework and finish it," Miss. Berrie said.

"Can we work with a partner?" a student asked.

"Yes, if you want to."

Wade and Lamman decided to work with each other and both completed their assignment. After class, wade went home, but before he left, he gave Lamman, Maxine and Sonya his phone number to keep in touch. Everybody exchange their phone numbers to each other to keep in touch.

"What you doin' when you get home?" Lamman asked.

"Relax a little bit before I go to work," wade said.

"I should do the same, I'll call you when I make it home," Lamman said.

"You got to go to work, don't you?" Wade asked.

"Not until four thirty, Lamman said. I'll call Sonya later on after work."

"Alright, I'll talk to you later, Wade said.

"Alright then," Lamman said.

Wade went home and layed in his bed and watched t.v. for a while. Five O' clock came and wade was at work. After he finished, he went home.

"How was school?" Lisa asked

"Fine," Wade responded.

"Nothing interesting happen?"

"No, not exactly, I just met up with Lamman and we both have the same classes all year long. I met all my teachers for today, I'll meet the others tomorrow and Maxine and I are a couple."

"Who is Maxine?" Lisa asked.

"Somebody I've known since ninth grade, she's pretty cool. She asked me to be her boyfriend and I said yes."

"Well you make sure you treat her right, there's no room in a relationship for nonesense," Lisa said.

"Yes Ma'am."

"Bring her over so I can meet her one day" , Lisa said.

"Yeah, I'll ask her." Wade said.

Wade picked up the phone to call Maxine and talk to her. Wade dialed her number and the phone ranged.

"Hello," Maxine answered.

"Maxine?" Wade said.

"Yes."

"This is Wade."

"Hey Wade, what you up to?"

"Nothing, I'm just calling you like I said I would, how you doing?" Wade asked.

"Watching t.v. and getting ready for tomorrow and my parents want to meet with you. When is the best time for you to come over?" Maxine asked.

"Probably Saturday afternoon. My mom wants to meet you too," Wade said.

"Really? I don't know when I can come over," Maxine said.

"Come by Saturday evening if you can," Wade said.

"Sure, that'll work."

"I'm gonna ask my mom can I swing by your house to meet your parents and I'll let you know when I see you at school," Wade said.

"O.K. me too, I'll ask my parents can I go by and meet your mother," Maxine said.

"Alright, I'll see you tomorrow Maxine, good night," Wade said.

"Good night Wade," Maxine said.

Wade hunged up the phone and went to bed.

Another Day At School

The next morning, Lisa left breakfast for Wade on the table and left for work. Wade woked up and got ready for school and ate breakfast. Once he arrived on school campus, he met up with his friends.

"What's up Wade?" Lamman said.

"What's goin' on?" Wade responded.

"Let's hang out over here, I told Sonya I'll be at this table where we sat yesterday so she can know where I'm at," Lamman said.

"You ready for today?" Wade ask smiling.

"You know it. Oh yeah, hey I almost forgot to tell you, check this out, I got my permit yesterday. That's why I forgot to call you yesterday, my momma took me to take the test as soon as I went home."

"Who gonna teach you to drive?" Wade asked.

"I don't know, but it doesn't matter, as long as I know how to drive, I don't care who teaches me."

A little while later, Maxine and Sonya had arrived at the school and met up with Wade and Lamman.

"Hey ya'll!" Sonya said smiling.

"Hey what's up Sonya?" Lamman said smilng back.

"What's going on Sonya?" Wade said smiling back.

"What's up Maxine?" they said back.

"So, what ya'll been up too? Sonya asked.

"Work," Wade said.

"Yeah, me too. I got my permit yesterday after school and I'm going to learn how to drive this weekend," Lamman said.

"Congratulations," Sonya said.

"Thank you," Lamman said.

"Here you go Maxine, these are my papers on poetry I told you about yesterday," Wade said.

"Yes, thank you, I'll give them back as soon as I finish."

The bell ranged and everyone went to class.

"I will see you at lunch!" Maxine said.

"Alright, I'll be waiting on ya," Wade said.

"Bye. Same place as yesterday right?" Maxine asked.

"Yeah," Wade responded.

"See you later," Sonya said.

"Alright," Lamman responded.

"C'mon, we got to go to P.E."

Wade and Lamman walked to the gym and met Coach Phillip.

"You two have a seat on the bleachers until the rest of the class gets here," Coach Phillip said.

Soon afterwards everybody arrive to class to begin their first lesson.

"Today we will do warm ups individually first and second with a partner. Everybody spread out to give yourself and others room to exercise. Everbody exerise for ten minutes by themselves and then with a partner.

Find a partner and a spot away from everybody else so you bump into one another," Coach Phillip said.

After gym class, Wade and Lamman was on their way to art class, but on the way to class, Wade had another confrontation with Mack who was coming down the hallway.

"Well, well, well look who it is, Mr. Pathetic," Mack said with a smirk on his face.

"Step aside Jimmy, I got a class to go to," Wade said.

"What class is that huh? a class for losers," Mack said and then started laughing.

"I don't have time to go back and forth with you and looking ignorant in front of all these people. It's too embarassing and too immature," Wade said.

"You callin' me ignorant?" Mack snapped.

Mack went face to face with Wade and the crowd gathered around to see.

"Get out of my face," Wade demanded.

"Make me punk," Mack said.

Security was coming, but before they could make it down the hall, Wade pushed Mack out of his face and Lamman grabbed Wade telling him let's go to class.

"C'mon Wade, he's not worth it," Lamman said.

Mack's crew grabbed him as well and went the opposite direction.

"What happened over here? Hey young man, come here."

Security called Mack before he got out of sight.

"What's going on here?"

"I got assaulted," Mack said.

"By who?" Security asked.

"By that punk, Wade Jackson."

"Come with me, we're going to the principal's office."

Security took Mack to the principal's office and he explained what had happen in the hallway. Then, the principal called Wade into her office to explained his side of the story.

"Jimmy tells me you pushed him, is that correct?" she asked.

"Yeah, but he wouldn't get out of my face talking trash," Wade said.

"Who started it?" the principal asked.

"He did, he's always bothering people," Wade said.

"If I see you two again, it'll be detention ot suspension for name calling, pushing, fighting or whatever you two do that's physical."

The principal let Wade go to class leaving him with a warning and the same fo Mack. Once Wade made it back to class, he explained everything to Lamman.

"A warning?!" Lamman said. You got to avoid any confrontations with Jimmy because who knows what might happen next."

The Fight

At lunch, Maxine can sense something was wrong with Wade.

"What's wrong Wade?" Maxine asked with a concern look on her face.

"I pushed Jimmy in the hallway earlier and the principal left us with a warning. I asked him to get out of my way, he wouldn't move so I pushed him," Wade explained.

"It's too early to fight right now, we're still in the first month of school. You need to avoid Jimmy so you won't get in trouble again," Maxine said.

"Easier said than done, I'll try to avoid him."

After lunch, Wade and Lamman went to third block.

"Last class of today," Lamman said with joy.

Once everybody arrived, class began.

"Hi everyone, I'm Mrs.Young and for this semester, we will learn ways to eat right and live healthy."

"What you got plan this weekend?" Lamman asked.

"Maxine's coming over to meet my mom. Since I told ma about her, she wants to meet her and I forgot to tell Maxine when I'm availiable to go over her house to meet her parents. If I see her before going home, I'll tell her or call her tonight and tell her." Wade explained

"I'm going on the road for my driving lessons with one of my parents. I don't know how long I'll be out there, driving looks easy, but is it easy?" Lamman said.

"I wouldn't know, I never got behind the wheel myself," Wade said.

"When you gonna try to get your permit?" Lamman asked.

"If I find some time, I can work on it this year."

Later on that day after Wade came home from work, Lisa wanted to talk about what happen at school.

"The principal called and told me what happened between you and some boy named Jimmy Sailor. You wanna explain what's going on?" Lisa asked with a mean look on her face.

"After P.E. class, I was on my way to art class, but before I could get there, for some reason Jimmy saw me and started blockin' my way and callin' me names. I had enough of him, so I pushed him. Then, security took both of us to the principal's office and she let go with a warning," Wade explained.

"Boy, don't you know it's too early to be fighting. School just opened back up this year and you and some other are already fighting. You aren't supposed to fight anyway, your supposed to learn and study to get a good education. Don't let this happen again," Lisa demanded.

"Alright," Wade said.

Later, Wade called Maxine.

"Hey Maxine, how you doing?" Wade asked.

"Hi Wade, I'm doing good, how are you?"

"I'll be alright, but listen, I think Sunday afternoon is the best time for me to come over and meet your parents. Is that o.k?" Wade asked.

"That'll be fine. I'll tell them what you said."

"Cool. So, how you'd like those poetry papers? were they good, o.k, alright or something?" Wade asked.

"I loved them, that poetry is good, it can make a person feel warm on the inside a good," Maxine said.

"I'm working on some more, don't know when I'll be finish though," Wade said.

"Wade? I'm worried about you," Maxine said.

"Why?"

"I'm concern that you might end up in a fight with Jimmy one day and I don't want that to happen."

"Don't worry, I won't fight him, I'll try to avoid him as much as I can," he said.

"You promise," Maxine said.

"Yes, for you, I promise."

"Thank you."

"I'm gonna let you go, I'll talk to you tomorrow," Wade said.

"Alright baby, see you tomorrow, bye," Maxine said.

"Baby?" Wade said to himself, I need to get use to calling her that as well."

A few weeks has passed at Emerson high school and everybody seems to be quiet about what happened that day between Wade and Mack. But then, another confrontation happened.

"Let me grab something to eat and I'll meet you outside," Maxine told Wade.

Once Wade made it outside, Mack approached him.

"Hey punk, don't think that I forgot what happen that day when you had the nerve to put your hands on me and got me in trouble," Mack said with anger.

"What you gonna do about it?" Wade asked.

The two went back and forth arguing and threatening each other. Then, Mack took a swing at Wade, but missed.

"Is that all you've got?" Wade asked.

Then Wade hit Mack with a blow to the stomach with his left hand and then acrossed the face with his right hand. Half the school students raned over to see the fight. Wade scooped Mack up and slammed him on the ground. Wade was dominating Mack in their first ever fight. It seems like Mack couldn't land one punch on Wade. As the fight continued, the crowd was roaring all the way until it was finished. Security was coming and then Wade spoked to a beat and battered Mack.

"Don't ever get in my face again, if you do, the second beatdown I'll give you will be a lot more painful than this."

Wade looked up at Mack's friends and spoked.

"What the HELL you people lookin' at? ya'll wanna do somethin' huh? ya'll don't like the fact that I whooped his ass? or should I say, dominate his punk ass. Ya'll wanna do somethin' about it? DO SOMETHIN', DO SOMETHIN', DO SOMETHIN I'll dare you, I'll dare you," Wade said angrily.

No one stepped up to fight Wade, fear must of went through their bodies. Security came and took Wade to the principal's office. Meanwhile, another Security officer helped Mack to the nurses office.

"Tell me what happen?" the principal asked Wade.

"Once again, Jimmy got in my face and started talking smack. Then, he tried to hit me," Wade said.

"So, what your saying is, he tried to hit you first?"

"Yes, he took the first swing, I fought back to defend myself, none of his friends didn't even try to stop him from fighting me. I didn't even want to fight," Wade said.

"I'll call Jimmy Sailor in to explain his side of the story after he's finish with the nurse. Meanwhile, I'm gonna have to suspend you for a week for fighting. Also, I'm gonna call your mother and tell her what took place outside at lunch. Is their any one who can come and pick you up? I think it's best if you went home right now before you end up in another fight." the principal asked.

"I can walk home, I only live like ten minutes away from the school," Wade said.

After the talk with the principal, Wade left the school and went straight home.

"Damn," Wade mumbled.

Later on that day when Wade came home from work, Lisa demanded to know what happened at school.

"The principal called me and explained what happen today at your school, what's going on?" Lisa asked.

"I don't know, I don't know why the guy picks on me when ever he see's me. His group of friends just laughs all the time at me when ever he starts calling me names."

"Who is this guy you talkin' about?"

"His name is Jimmy Sailor, his friends calls him Mack and he plays football for the school."

"Are you the only one he picks on?"

"No, there are others, but it seems like I'm the only one, it just seems that way. He's been picking on me since I started high school, day by day, week by week, month by month and year by year. Until today, I had enough, I couldn't take it much longer, I tried to be a nice guy by not fighting him, but no, he just had to push it."

"If you were having trouble out of this guy, why didn't you say something?" Lisa asked.

"I really didn't think it'll go this far and what good will telling on him do? that's not going to solve anything, you'll still get picked on. I never been suspended before until now in my last year in high school."

"It wouldn't have happen if you have ignored that guy and tried to avoid him when you see him. You ignored him in all those other years right? why stop now?" Lisa asked.

"I don't know, I guess enough was enough," Wade said.

"I'm still in disbelief, Lisa said. What are you going to around the house all week?"

"I don't know, nothing is coming to mind right now. I'm still in disbelief myself about what had happen at school. I guess I can't go over Maxine's house to meet her parents huh?" Wade asked.

"No, not right now, I don't want them to know your suspended. Who knows what they might say about you or think of you," Lisa said.

"Does Maxine or any of your friends know about that fight? have they seen it?"

"I don't know, if they've seen it, I didn't see them because there were a lot of people outside. I'm sure they've heard about it, nothing stays quiet around that school. Your business will get put out before school is over for today."

After the talk with his mother, Wade went to his room and he still was angry about being suspended for a full week. Then, his phone ranged.

"Hello," he answered.

"What happened at school today?" Maxine said with anger.

"What's wrong with you? you seem tense" Wade said.

"Why shouldn't I be? now, answered the question."

"Mack got in my face again and he tried to hit me."

"What else?" Maxine asked.

"I kicked his ass and got suspended for a week."

"A week?!" Maxine said.

"Yeah, I didn't even start this fight, he came towards me and tried to nail me."

"So your sayin' he just walked towards you out of nowhere and tried to hit you? I take it that you didn't say anything to provoke him," Maxine said.

"Well, we didn't fight until after we got through talking trash about one another. He started it though."

"What now, Wade?" Maxine asked.

"I got to stay home and wait out this suspension," Wade said.

"Why doesn't Jimmy like you?" Maxine asked.

"Don't know and don't give a damn," Wade said.

"Try not to run into him again o.k?" Maxine said.

"Now that I've whooped his ass, he should be avoiding me, not me avoiding him."

"I don't want you to get hurt again," Maxine said.

"I'll be alright."

"Just think about what I said and then you truly be alright. Well, I'll talk to you tomorrow to see how things are going. Yeah, talk to you later, bye."

"Bye," Wade responded.

They both hunged up the phone and Wade is still angry about the whole suspension situation.

Suspension Days

"While I'm on suspension, I can use this week to take my driving test. I already studied, I just haven't took the test yet."

That Monday morning after Lisa left for work, Wade got on the city bus to go take his driving test. A few hours later, Wade arrived at the driver testing office. Now, the pressure was on once he started his exam. In the end, he manage to pass and was glad that he did.

"I'm gonna keep quiet about this for awhile just to surprise everyone."

Later on that day when Lisa came home, she wanted another conversation with Wade.

"The principal called me and she said that you were telling the truth about that guy Jimmy. He told the principal the what happened, his story was the same as yours. Your principal suspended him for two weeks," Lisa explained.

"Oh yeah! really? two weeks? I thought I had it bad," Wade said.

"I'm still disappointed in you for fighting, but I'm happy that you told the truth," Lisa said.

"So, how was work?"

"Fine, same thing everyday though," he responded.

"Your not doing anything you shouldn't be doing that'll get you fired are you?" Lisa asked.

"No, I'm just doing the usual."

"So, what are your thoughts on turning eighteen?"

"It feels good, I can finally purchase a few items that I couldn't buy without a parent approval. I can finally do just about whatever I want," Wade said.

"Your not drinking are you? or doing drugs? or both?" Lisa asked.

"No, why would I risk my life doing drugs or drinking alcohol? it's too dangerous to me," Wade said.

"Good, I don't want to put you out of my house for dealing with drugs or alcohol. I'm goin' to let you go, I gotta get ready for tomorrow anyway, good night," Lisa said.

Lisa leaned over and gave Wade a kiss on the fore head. Then the phone ranged.

"Hello," Wade said.

"What's up Wade?" Lamman said.

"Hey, what's going on?" Wade responded.

"Nothin' much, same thing everyday, I thought about callin' you a lot sooner, but I thought maybe you didn't want to talk to anybody after what happened between you Jimmy," Lamman said.

"You seen the fight?" Wade asked.

"No, it was over before I got outside, I just heard about it."

"What did you hear? most students could be lying about the story?"

"They said you beat his ass down to the ground by yourself," Lamman explained.

"That's true, none of his friends didn't even helped him out either, I guess they didn't want none," Wade said.

"I've heard about that too, they said they didn't want Jimmy to look weak by fighting one person. You know, Jimmy and one of his friends versus you and only you."

I'm still hanging in there though, I come back next week," Wade said.

"I'll see you then and I'll hear from you tomorrow, I gotta go."

"Alright then, talk to you later," Wade said.

The next morning Wade went to driving school to learn to drive. He stayed for a couple of hours and was starting to understand how to operate a vehicle.

"I'll be back for more lessons tomorrow, Thursday and Friday," Wade told his instructor.

"Then, so on, Wade continued to practice driving so he can be a good and safe driver. Now that he's finish learning, he needs a car to obtain his license.

"I know someone I could asked," Wade said.

Wade then called his uncle Kurt and explained everything to him. Kurt then decided to let Wade have the car since Kurt couldn't make it on Wade's birthday because of work and plus he likes trucks than cars. Wade was excited and rushed over to pick up the car. Afterwards, he drove back state police office to take his skills test. After a few hours on the road, the driving examiner told Wade he'd passed thethe skill test. So, Wade went and took his picture to show on his driver's license card.

"All I need now is insurance of my own and I'll be o.k."

He then drove to progressive to talk about insurance plans and after everything was explained to him, he agreed to have progressive insurance. Everything was settled and Wade then drove to work later on that day. After work, Lisa had a few questions for Wade.

Who's car is that? and why is it in my driveway?"

"It was uncle Kurt's, but he let me have it as a late birthday present," Wade said.

"Who taught you how to drive?" she asked.

"I went to this driving school after I got my permit. I only went there for a few days. It started off hard, but the more I practice, the more easier driving became," Wade said.

"What about insurance? you can't drive anywhere without that," Lisa asked.

"I'm with progressive, I was over there today."

"So, you did all this in one day?"

"I got the car first, second, I took the skills test and third, I bought some insurance right after I took my picture for my license card," Wade explained.

"I hade nothing else to do this week, that's why I came up with this plan."

"Congratulations," Lisa said with joy.

"Thank you," he said.

"And please be careful driving and please follow the rules on the road. We don't need you in an accident." Lisa said.

Chapter 12

Back To School

"Welcome back bro, you missed out on a lot. I'll fill you in on it later, come with me," Lamman said.

They both walked outside to the student parking lot and Lamman showed Wade his car.

"It's a two thousand Toyota Camry, I got this from car-mart with my dad's help and my savings from my job," he said.

"That's nice, do you have insurance?" Wade asked.

"I got all state insurance," Lamman responded.

"When did you actually get this car? it looks pretty good ya know."

"Tell you the truth, I had it for three days, I haven't said anything about it because I wanted to make sure that it's in good condition and everything is working properly," Lamman explained.

"I got my own ride too, I had it since Friday," Wade said.

"Where?" Lamman asked.

"Over here, C'mon."

"It's a pontiac grand prix GT, two thousand one model, nice really," Wade said.

"When and how did you get this, this is not a bad car, it's nice," Lamman said.

"I got this last week from my uncle as a late birthday present. I took my test first to get my permit and went back to take my skills test to get my license, but in between I went to driving school to learn to drive. I got my license right here with me. Driving is pretty much easy, I thought it might be hard on how you suppose to operate it. I guess I was wrong, but now I can drive to work everyday and school instead of walking," Wade explained.

"That's true. Do Maxine know about it?" Lamman asked.

"No, not yet, I want to surprise her. Is she even here?" Wade asked.

"Don't know, I haven't seen her just yet," Lamman responded.

"Let's go inside," Wade said.

"Hey Wade, hi Lamman," Sonya said while walking up to them.

"Wade? are you o.k? I heard what happened between you and Jimmy," Sonya asked.

"Yeah, I'm alright, I just need to catch up on my assignments that I missed while on suspension."

"I never thought that you would end up in a fight and also get suspended," she said.

"Yeah, I didn't think I would fight somebody either and win," Wade said.

"Hey ya'll, Maxine said.

"Hey, we were looking for you too, we thought you didn't show up today," Lamman said.

"Can I have a word with you?" Maxine asked Wade.

"No problem, Sonya, Lamman we'll be right back."

Wade and some group of kids were talking while Wade and Maxine were walking outside.

"We heard what happened and we think it was cool on how you defended yourself against a guy like Jimmy. We think if you can beat him, so can one of us," a student said.

"All of you were getting picked on by Jimmy?" Maxine asked.

"Yeah, but not lately though," another student said.

"What grade are you guys in?" Maxine asked.

"Ninth grade," a girl said.

"Is it just Jimmy whose been picking on you all or are there more?" Wade asked.

"Some of his friends like to embarrass us when ever they can," the boy said.

"How long have this been going on?" Maxine asked.

"Awhile," the girl said.

"It's best if you all just leave those guys alone, just ignore them. They'll be out of your lives forever once they graduate or if they graduate. Neither one of them isn't worth gettin' suspended over towards the last few weeks in school, but I know where you all are coming from with this. I fought Jimmy 'cause he's been on my ass since ninth grade and this year was goin' to be different. I had enough of his big mouth," Wade explained.

"Just take my advice, concentrate on what you all got to do to pass the ninth grade and just ignore those fools, they don't know what there talking about when they talk dirty towards you all."

"Your right, they ain't worth it, I just wonder how they will survive in the real world acting the way they act towards people," the boy said.

"Well, they may not get far for the rest of their lives," the girl said.

"Hey, thanks for the advice Wade, we appreciate it," the boy said.

After the talk with the ninth graders, Wade and Maxine went outside to talk.

"How you doing? you gonna be alright after what happen?" Maxine asked.

"Yeah, I'll be fine. I just want to put all this behind me and just move on with life," Wade said.

"I'm so glad to hear that," Maxine said with joy.

"Oh yeah! come with me over here, I want to show you something."

"So, what do you think?" he asked.

"Oh my god! Wade? how did you afford this?" Maxine asked with a surprise look.

"I didn't buy it, my uncle gave it to me as a late birthday present. I got my license and insurance for it too."

"You think we can go out sometime in it?" Maxine asked.

"Yeah, we can go for a ride probably anytime. I can tell by the look on your face that you like this car," Wade said smiling.

"Yeah, it's a beautiful car. Everything seems like it's in good condition," Maxine said.

"Everythings fine, it's already been checked out by my uncle," Wade said.

"We don't have anything to worry about once we hit the road," Wade said.

Chapter 13

The future

"Hello," Wade answered the phone.

"What up Wade?" Lamman said. You goin' to school dance? or do you got other plans?"

"When is it exactly?" Wade asked.

"It's Friday night at eight thirty p.m."

"Me and Sonya going, she's riding with me though just to let you know," Lamman said.

"I'll ask Maxine if she wants to go, but hey, is it this Friday or next Friday or do we got three weeks until then?"

"Yeah, actually it's next Friday," Lamman said.

"Good, it just gives me time to find and buy a suit," Wade said.

"I got mine already just to get it out of the way so I won't worry about it later. I gotta go, I'll talk to you tomorrow," Lamman said.

"Alright then," Wade said.

The next day at school, Wade went up and asked Maxine to the school dance.

"You doing anything next Friday night Maxine?" Wade asked.

"No, I don't have anything plan, why?"

"You want to go to the school dance with me?"

Maxine blushed, she was excited that Wade asked her out to the dance.

"Yes, I'll go out with you, but what should I wear? I need to go shopping this weekend," she said.

"I'm free this weekend, I'll take you shopping if you want me to," Wade said.

"Thank you baby, I appreciate it," Maxine said with loving care.

Maxine leaned over and gave Wade a kiss. Once Saturday came, Wade and Maxine were off to shopping.

"I know a good place where we could shop, it's not too far from here actually," Maxine said.

"Here we are."

"Paradise?" Wade said.

"Yeah, it's a good place for us girls to shop, get our hair done, get a manicures and pedicures. It's sort of like a mall except this store is for women," she said.

They got out of the car and went inside." It looks nice in here," Maxine said.

"Ya don't say," Wade said.

For a few hours, Maxine shop to find the perfect dress and after she found it, she bought it and took it home.

"This is what I wanted, it's beautiful," she said.

"Yeah, it is, hey, how bout a movie later on today if your not busy," Wade said.

"What did you have in mind?" Maxine said.

"An Action Adventure kind of movie."

"Let me check my schedule and I'll call you to let you know something," Maxine said.

Later that day, they both went to the movies and had a good time.

"That movie was good, I rather like it. Thanks for bringing me here Wade!" Maxine said with joy.

"Tomorrow's another beautiful day, you wanna do something else?" Maxine asked.

"You have something in mind?" Wade asked.

"Yep, a picnic at the park would be nice," Maxine said.

"Sure, why not? I never been on a picnic before anyway," Wade said smiling.

"Really?" she asked.

"Yeah, it never comes to mind, ya know? I seen people on picnics, but I never been on one," Wade explained.

"Once you experience being or should I say going on a picnic, you'll love it, its fun," Maxine explained.

"Here we are, home sweet home, well I'll see you tomorrow."

"Alright, I'll call you later," Wade said.

"Promise?" she asked with a smile.

"Yeah, I promise," he said smiling.

They both leaned over and gave each other a kiss. Later, Wade called Maxine and talked about everything that they could think of. Then, the next day Wade went over and picked up Maxine to go on their picnic.

"This park is huge! look at all this space, isn't this nice?" Maxine said with excitement.

"Yeah, it is," Wade responded.

Then, they took out their food to eat and started talking to get to know one another a little bit better.

"Let's bond, tell me something that I don't know about you already," Maxine said.

"I grew up here in Arkansas and my mother raised me by herself. I don't know much about my daddy, he didn't bother to stick around long before I was born. My mom is a nurse, she is the only one who looked out for me all my life. I got picked on about my weight ever since I started school and I was ugly, at least that's what they said. It's been bothering me, but i didn't start losing weight just because they were picking on me, I lost it because it was bad for my health. I never was popular, I guess that's why I never been on dates, but I didn't care, I didn't let that bother me too much. I just stayed focus on my studies and that's why I made it to the twelve grade."

"I'm so sorry, I didn't know you went through all that," Maxine said with a concern look.

"All that is in the past and I'll just leave it there," Wade said.

"Tell me something about you that I may not know already Maxine."

"Well, I grew up in Baltimore where my parents got married. Things were o.k until my dad got layed off work. Things got hard, but we survive it though because my dad got a spot on the police force. My mother is lawyer, she went to Harvard law school. They both work here in Arkansas, that's why we live here now. I used to work as a salesperson in lady footlocker. The payment was good and I rather like it. I've been in some bad relationships before, the guy didn't treat me the way he suppose to. He didn't hit me though, but he did cheated on me with another girl. My heart was broken, I never spoke to him again and probably never will."

"He broke your heart? what the hell was he thinking?" Wade asked.

"Some people in life aren't as good as they may seem, ya know?" Maxine said.

"That's true, I agree."

Friday came and Wade picked up Maxine and headed off to the school dance.

"Wow, you look stunning, I mean absolutely stunning," Wade said once he saw Maxine in her dress.

"Thank you, you look handsome in your suit," Maxine said smiling.

"Appreciate it," Wade responded.

Once they arrived, they met up with Sonya and Lamman.

"What's up ya'll," Lamman said.

"Hey, what up," Wade responded.

"Girl you look so cute in your dress," Maxine said to Sonya.

"Thank you, so do you," Sonya said.

"Let's go in and have fun," Lamman said.

Wade, Maxine, Sonya and Lamman dance the night away and had a good time.

A few weeks later, Wade invited Maxine over for dinner so that she and his mother can get to know each other. In a few moments the door bell ranged.

"Hi Wade," Maxine said with a smile.

"Hi, thanks for coming over, come on in," he said.

"Maxine, this is my mom Lisa, mom, this is Maxine."

"Hi Maxine, good to finally meet you," Lisa said.

"Thank you, same here, good to meet you," Maxine responded.

"You like little caesars pizza Maxine?" Wade asked.

"Yeah, I love it," she said.

"Alright, everythings ready, you two can eat," Lisa said.

"How is Wade treating you?" Lisa asked.

"With respect and love," she responded.

"What kind of question is that?" Wade said with a smile.

"I told Wade to never hit a girl or disrespect her, no matter what happens." Lisa said.

"So far, he's been kind, he took me shopping for a new dress for the school dance," Maxine said.

"That's good, but what about the prom? did ya'll ever think about going?" Lisa asked.

"I'm going, I need to shop for another dress, what about you Wade? are you going to the prom?" Maxine asked.

"Yeah, I'm going. I already have a suit for the prom, Lamman and I bought one while we were hanging out one day. So, I'm all set," Wade said.

"You never told me about that," Lisa said.

"Yeah, I know, I forgot," Wade said.

"Where you going to buy another dress?" Wade dress thaid.

"Same place as last time, I saw another pretty dress that I like," Maxine said.

"What place is this?" Lisa asked.

"It's called paradise, a store for just women to shop around or get your hair done, manicures, pedicures, all types of stuff?" Maxine explained.

"Ma, whenever you get the chance, you should go over there and check it out, you may like it," Wade said.

"It's getting late, I should be on my way home," Maxine said.

"I'll drive you home if you want," Wade said.

"Alright, nice meeting you, Lisa," she said.

"Same here, come back anytime you like, o.k?" Lisa said.

Wade and Maxine left the house and got in the car and drove off.

"Your mother's nice."

"Yeah, she is."

"We're here, I'll see you later, o.k?" Maxine said.

"Alright, good night," Wade responded.

Prom night was coming up and every senior was excited to go.

"Prom night is Friday, you still going?" Lamman asked.

"You know it, I can't miss this night," Wade said.

"Can you take me to go buy my new dress after school today?" Maxine asked.

"Yeah, I'll take you, Wade said.

"You won't be late for work will you?" she asked.

"I don't go in until five o' clock, so no," Wade responded.

"Sonya already got everything she wanted, so we're good to go," Lamman said.

Friday came and everybody was at the prom having a good time. They spent the whole night dancing, talking, laughing and eating. Everything was was nice.

The next week, Wade was excited, graduation was almost here. Once he made it to school, he met up with Sonya.

"Hey Sonya" , he said.

"Hi Wade, what you doing?" she asked.

"Nothing, I just got here. You ready for graduation?" Wade asked.

"Yeah, I'm so excited. I've been waiting on this day for a long time."

"You and me both. I can't wait, I'm ready."

"You took your exams already?" Sonya asked.

"Yep, I took all of them. Some was easy, others was hard."

"What's up ya'll?" Lamman said.

"Where you been? we were waiting for you," Sonya asked.

"I just got here."

"We were talking about graduation day," Wade said.

"Man, I can't wait for that day to get here. I'm ready for it, I got my cap and gown already."

"You seen Maxine?" Sonya asked.

"I saw her go in the guidance counselor office," Lamman said.

"So, what ya'll got going on after graduation?" Wade asked.

"I'm going to college next year during the fall. Since I'm graduating this year, I'm trying to kick back for awhile for the rest of the year really before I start college," Lamman explained.

"I'm going to college with my man Lamman, we're a team, we have each others backs no matter what," Sonya said.

"I know that's right. What you doing Wade?" Lamman asked.

"I'm thinking about joining the Navy and doing auto technology while I'm in there."

"When you plan on taking the practice test?" Sonya asked.

"Probably later this year. I'm like Lamman, I wanna kick back and relax for awhile too."

"Hey ya'll," Maxine said.

"Maxine? what you doing after high school?" Lamman asked.

"I'm going to college next year with you guys."

"Cool, we can see each other everyday," Lamman said.

A week later, graduation day was here and everybody was ready.

"Ma, you ready to go?" Wade asked.

"Yeah, come on, I'll drive," Lisa said.

"How do you feel now that your graduating?" she asked.

"It feels great. I worked hard at school ever since I started, just to get to this point and time despite the trouble that followed," he said.

"And I'm thinking about joining the Navy later this year, but in the mean time, I just want to relax."

"What do you mean by relax?" Lisa asked.

"Relax a little bit from all this work, like school work and work from my job, but since I'm graduating, I don't have to worry about school work no more."

"I'm proud of you Wade, good job," Lisa said while smiling.

"Thank you."

Once they arrive at the graduation ceremony, everybody got in line to receive their diploma and some received scholarships.

"You got a scholarship?" Wade asked.

"Yep, to the University of Arkansas at Little Rock. It's a full scholarship too, I'm gonna play basketball while I'm there," Lamman said.

"Congratulations baby, give me a kiss," Sonya said to Lamman happily.

"I got a scholarship too see, I'm so happy," she said.

"I also got a scholarship too see," Maxine said with a smile.

"Congradulations." Wade said.

"Thank you." Maxine responded happily.

"Can I get a kiss?" Maxine asked.

"Yes, you may," Wade responded.

"Congratulations honey," Maxine's mom said.

"Thank you, oh yeah, mom, dad this is Wade, Wade, these are my parents."

"Hi, how you doing?" Wade said.

"How you doing young man?" Maxine's father and Mother said.

"What do you have plan after graduation? Maxine's mother asked.

"I'm joining the Navy to study auto technology," Wade said.

"That's good news young man, go for it," Maxine's father said.

"Mom, dad, can I speak with Wade along for a few minutes?" Maxine asked.

"Sure, we'll be right over here."

"I'm sad that your going off to the Navy. I been thinking that I'll never see you again something dangerous might happen to you," Maxine said with a worried look.

"Maxine, you'll hear from me, I'll send you emails and text messages to let you know how I'm doing, I'll come back for a visit," Wade explained.

Maxine hugged Wade.

"I promise I'll wait for you," she said.

"I'll wait for you too," Wade said.

"I don't want to be like that guy who broke your heart, I love you too much."

"I love you too Wade," Maxine said.

"Did you ever get your car from your parents for your birthday or Christmas?" Wade asked.

"No, I got it for a graduation present instead. I can why it took a long time, it's a two thousand six cadillac CTS. It is so beautiful, I'll show it to you after we leave here."

"Well, you did worked hard this whole year, so you deserve it," Wade said.

"Thank you, your so sweet."

"Let me get a picture of you baby," Lisa said.

"Alright, can Maxine be in it too and my other friends?"

"Sure, come on."

Everybody gathered around to take a picture to remember that day forever. Then, the principal got on stage to make one more announcement.

"Congratulations to all our seniors who received a scholarship and good luck with your journey to be successful and good luck in the future. God bless you all, good job everybody."

"And that's my story, it's been a long ride. I had bad, bad, bad days and I had really good days. I hope that my future is as bright as I envisioned it."